FARAH'S NOSE

A celebration of
South Asian heritage and family

Humera Malik

Chaaya Prabhat

Farah POKED and PRODDED.

She **squeezed** and **pinched**.

HMPH!

Farah turned to the **left**.

She turned to the **right**.

But it was no use.
No matter what she did or how she looked at it, all Farah could see was a big nose.

"I love your nose," Baba said.
"And every bit of you from your head to your toes."

Farah sighed.

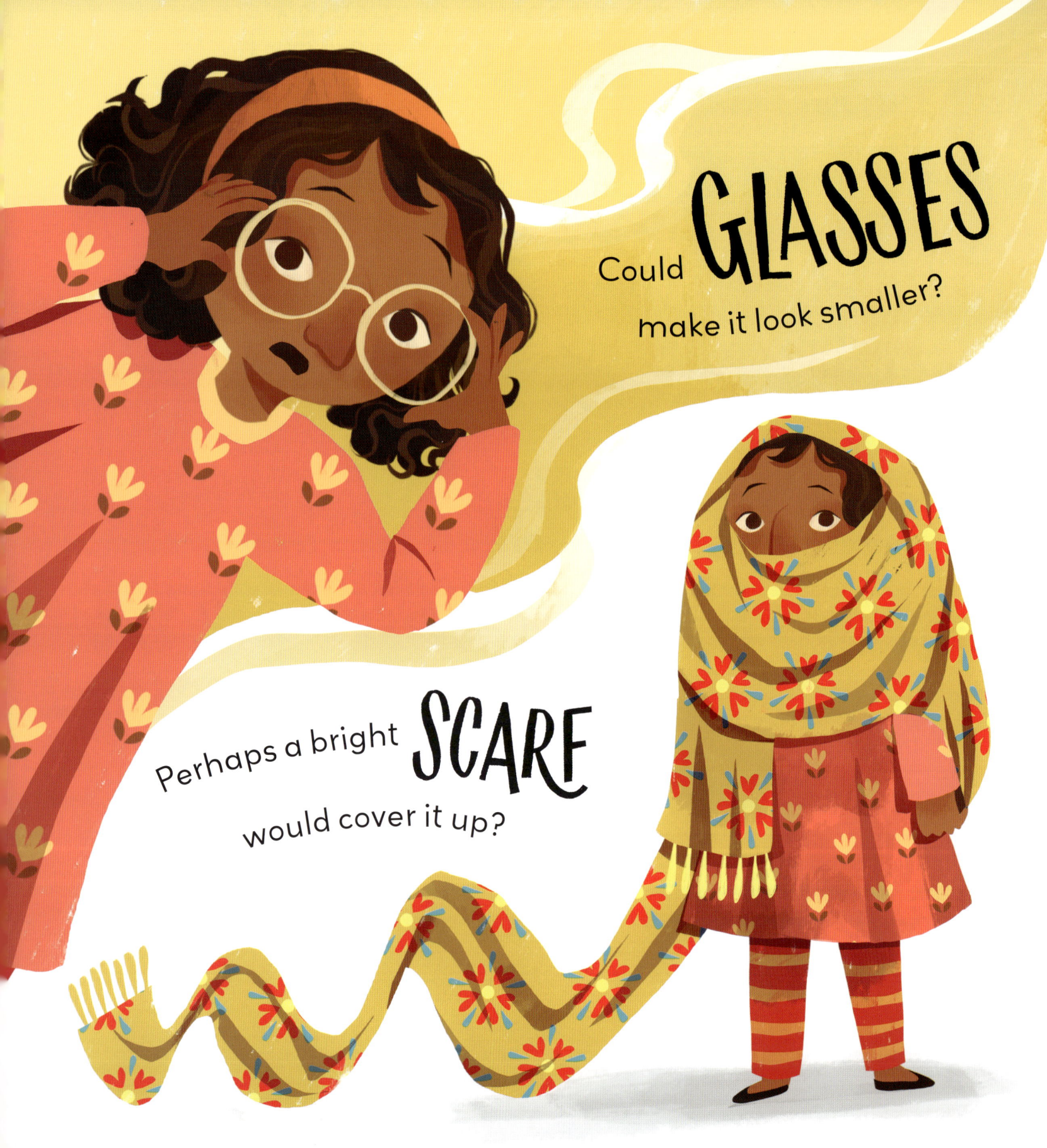

Maybe a **diamond** could make it SPARKLE?

But nothing worked.

"You have a STRONG nose," Mama said.

Farah did not understand.
How can a **nose** be strong, Farah wondered.

Farah couldn't help but examine her nose whenever she saw her reflection.

In the **mirror**.

In **windows**.

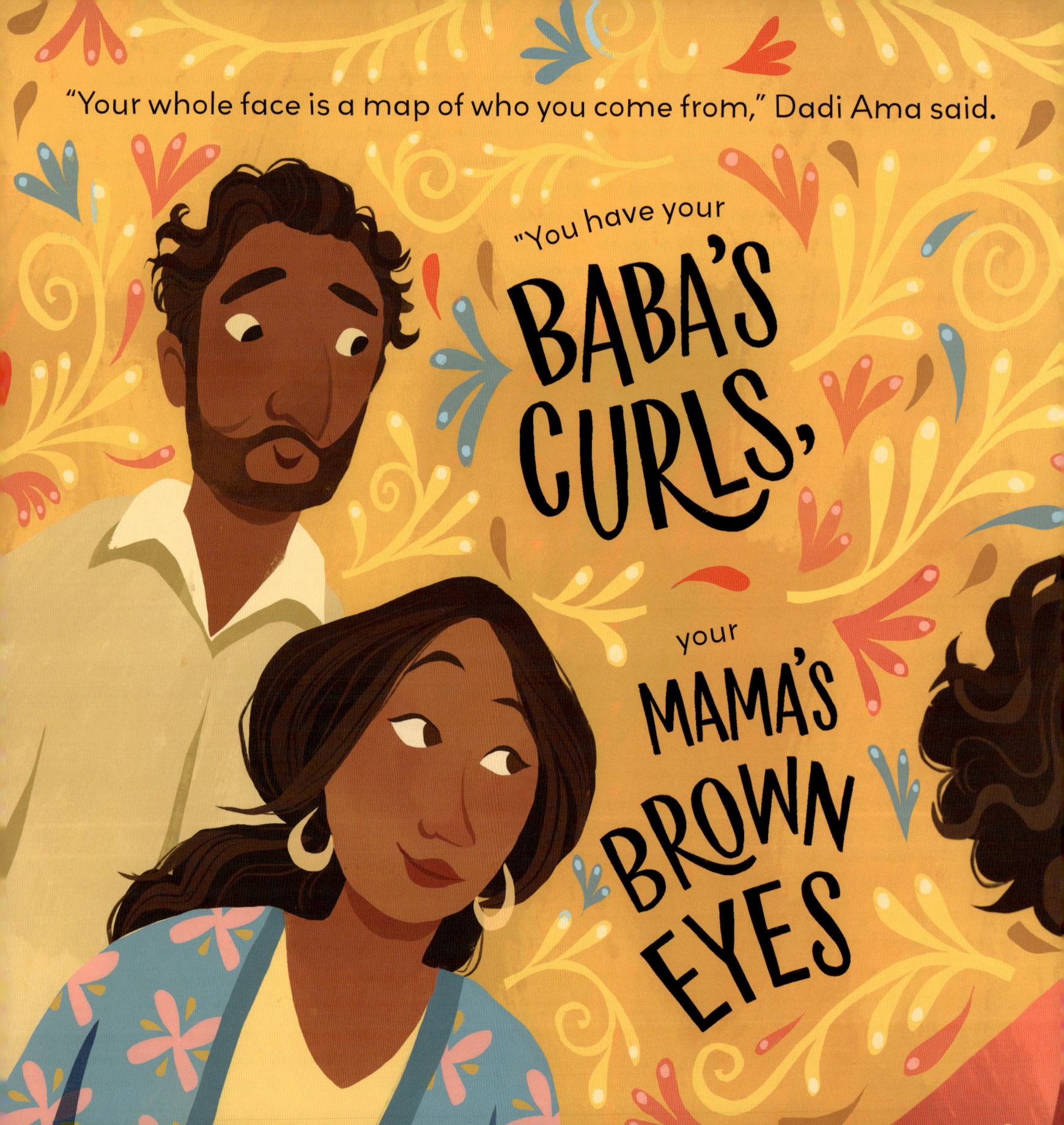

"Your whole face is a map of who you come from," Dadi Ama said.

"You have your

BABA'S CURLS,

your MAMA'S BROWN EYES

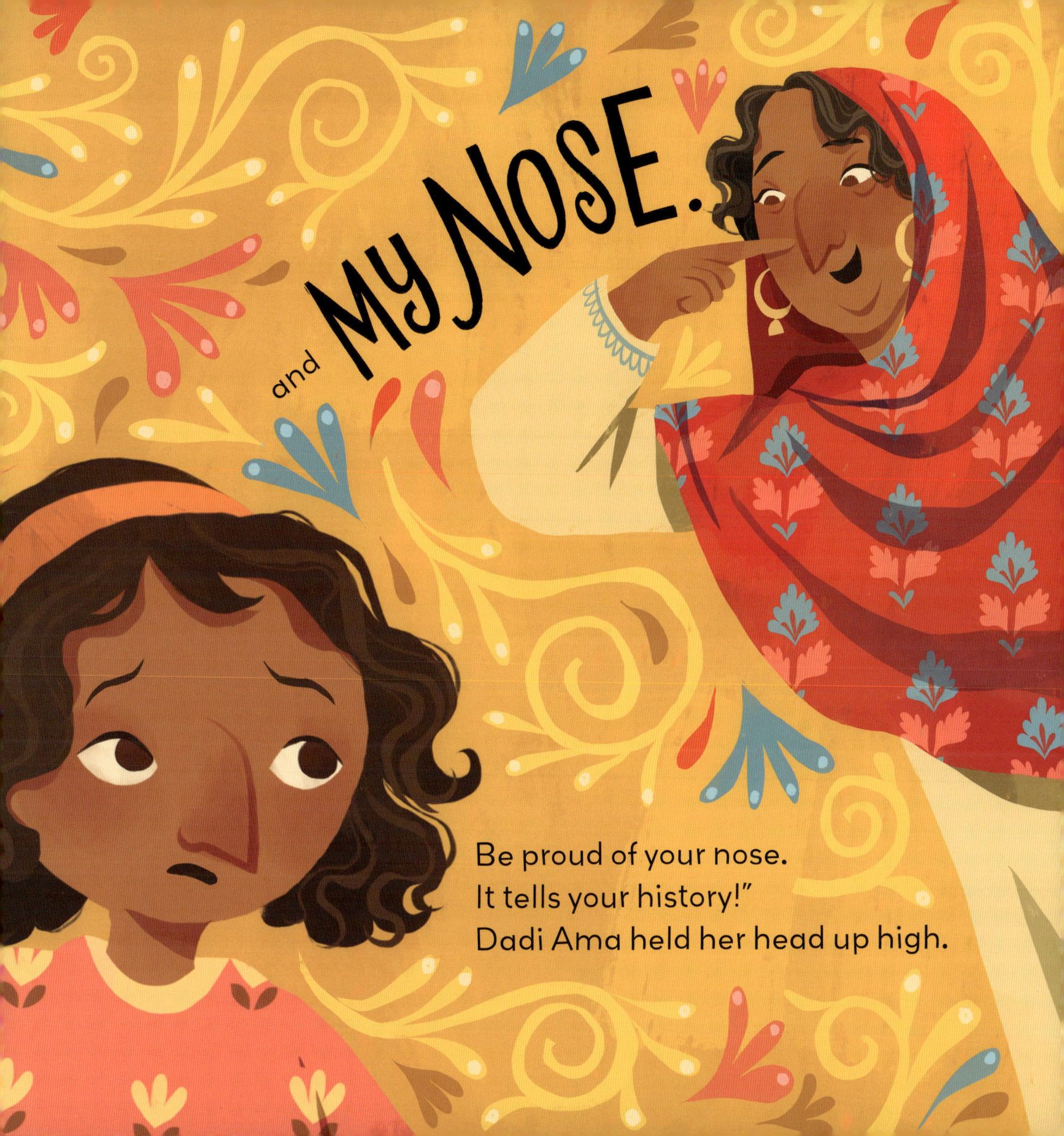

and MY NOSE.

Be proud of your nose.
It tells your history!"
Dadi Ama held her head up high.

Then, on her way home, Farah spotted **her nose**,

on a lady,

on a poster,

on a bus.

That afternoon, Farah asked to go to the exhibition.

"Welcome!" the museum curator said.

She showed Farah how to read the story behind each picture.

Immigration is moving to a new country. People who move to a new country are called immigrants.

They helped their children feel at home in new lands where some people did not think they belonged.

At first, South Asians didn't have many options for work. In some factories, South Asians comprised 90 per cent of the workers.

and **worked hard** to help provide for their families.

Farah saw her nose on the faces of the **proud** women who wore their salwar kameez and cooked their **traditional dishes** because they wanted their children to remember where they came from.

When South Asians first moved to new countries, the ingredients for their dishes weren't always available. Now, these spices, ingredients and dishes are found around the world.

Many proudly **shared their culture**, until their new friends and neighbours came to embrace it too.

Farah saw her nose on the faces of the **selfless** women who **helped others** from their homeland and their new home, with kindnesses big and small,

All of the major religions of South Asia emphasise the importance of charity: Zakat in Islam, Seva in Sikhism and Dana in Hinduism.

until they became the heart of their community.

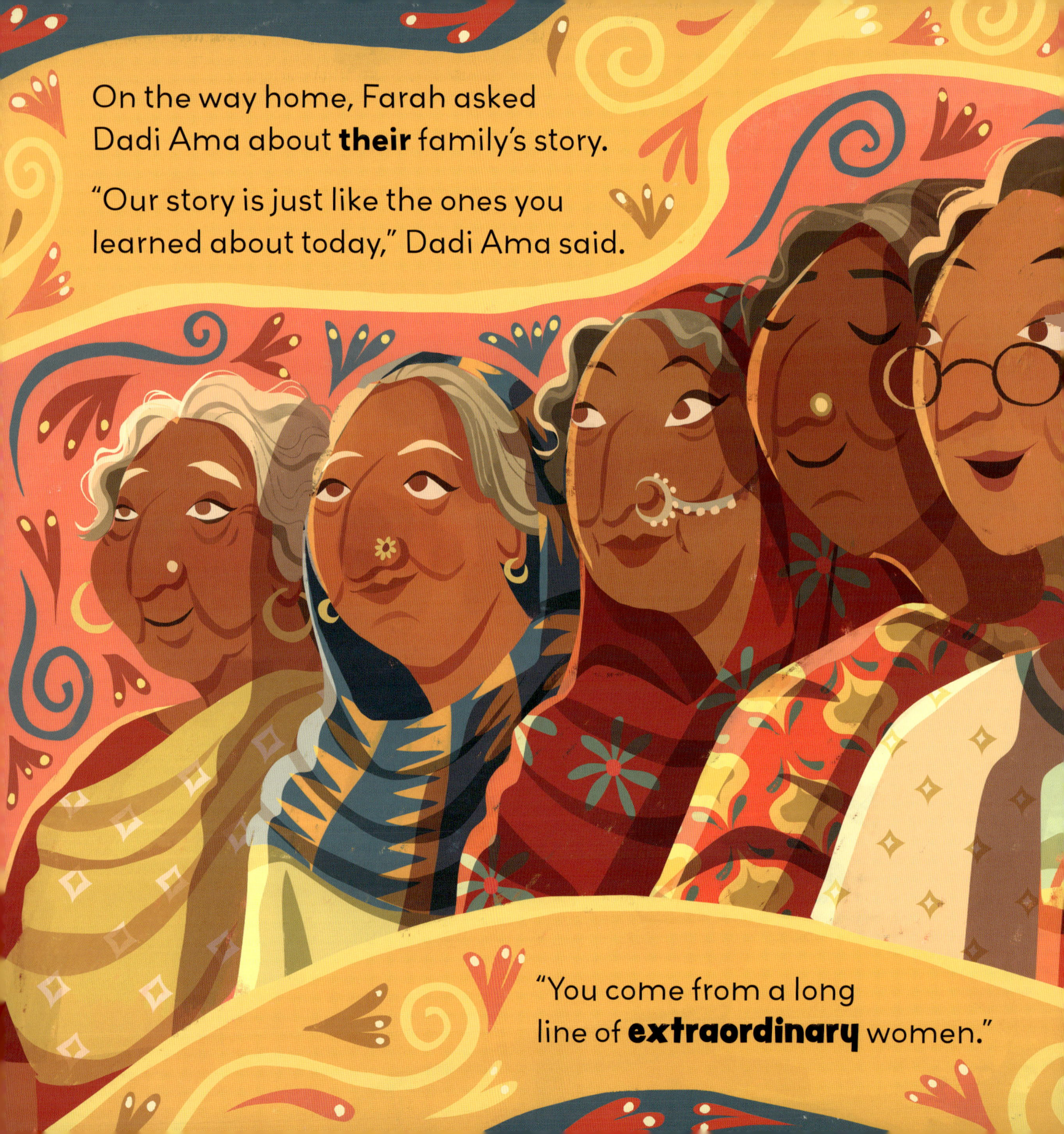

On the way home, Farah asked Dadi Ama about **their** family's story.

"Our story is just like the ones you learned about today," Dadi Ama said.

"You come from a long line of **extraordinary** women."

Farah now understood what it meant to have a strong nose. As she looked at the map of her face, she saw **her** history.

She turned to the left and she turned to the right.

She held her head up high.

Throughout the twentieth century, South Asians immigrated to new lands to build new lives for themselves and their children.

The women worked hard both inside and outside the home, yet their contributions and sacrifices often went unnoticed and their stories went untold. These ladies — among them my own elders — made sure that their children knew and felt proud of their religion and culture, and that they understood the importance of generosity and service to others.

I can say from my own experience that it is not easy growing up when you look different from most of the people around you, but there is beauty in our differences. I hope this story helps young girls to see themselves in the women who came before them, and learn to love every little bit of themselves, and in doing so, be more accepting of others.

Your friend,

Humera Malik

For the strong women who raised me, most of all, Ami and Nani
– H.M.

HODDER CHILDREN'S BOOKS
First published in Great Britain in 2025 by
Hodder & Stoughton Ltd

1 3 5 7 9 10 8 6 4 2

Text copyright © Humera Malik, 2025
Illustrations copyright © Chaaya Prabhat, 2025

Humera Malik and Chaaya Prabhat have asserted their right under the Copyright, Designs and Patents Act 1988, to be identified as the author and illustrator respectively of this work.
All rights reserved.
A CIP catalogue record for this book is available from the British Library.

PB ISBN 978-1-44497-661-8
E-book ISBN 978-1-44497-662-5

Printed in China

To my fellow long, pointy, hook-nosed people
– C.P.

Hodder Children's Books
An imprint of Hachette Children's Group
Part of Hodder & Stoughton Limited
Carmelite House
50 Victoria Embankment
London, EC4Y 0DZ

An Hachette UK Company
www.hachette.co.uk
www.hachettechildrens.co.uk

The authorised representative in the EEA is Hachette Ireland, 8 Castlecourt Centre, Dublin 15, D15 XTP3, Ireland (email: info@hbgi.ie)